This book belongs to
tired parents, grandparents,
and children everywhere,
especially:

_____

For Patricia, Daniela, Alice, Sam, Cat,
Hannah, Jenny, Debs, Daria, Miri, and all
the other mums who have kept me sane!
—KB

Dozy Bear and the Secret of Sleep
Text copyright © 2016 by Katie Blackburn
Illustrations copyright © 2016 by Richard Smythe

www.harpercollinschildrens.com

ISBN 978-0-06-256426-9 (trade bdg.)

Typography by Chelsea C. Donaldson

16 17 18 19 20   SCP   10 9 8 7 6 5 4 3 2 1
❖
First U.S. edition, 2017
Originally published in the UK by Faber and Faber, 2016

DOZY BEAR
and the
SECRET
of SLEEP

Katie Blackburn

Illustrated by
Richard Smythe

HARPER
An Imprint of HarperCollinsPublishers

Now, are you ready for bed?
Snuggle up and I will tell you a story
about a little bear called Dozy,
who wanted to sleep
but didn't know how.

Every night, Dozy Bear climbed
into his cozy den, ready for bed,
and his eyes would droop,
and his head would feel *heavy*,
and he'd feel ready to sleep.
He'd think of all the other
animals, *fast asleep*. . . .

The monkeys, tucked away in the trees, sleeping.

The hippos, cuddling in the mud, sleeping.

The birds, high up in their nests, sleeping.

The giraffes, their long necks curled, sleeping.

The zebras, cozied up back
to back, sleeping.

The elephants softly snoring, sleeping.
And Dozy Bear wondered: Was there a secret to sleeping?

His mama yawned. *Ah ahhhh.*
"Little one, there is no secret to sleeping," she said.
"You just wait for sleep to come.
See how dark it is. Dark, dark everywhere.
Feel how sleepy you are. As sleepy as can be.
Now, close your eyes and snuggle down,
and very, very soon you will sleep too."

And Dozy sighed, *Ah ahhhh.*
And he snuggled down.
And he waited and he waited
and he waited. But he did not
fall asleep.

Papa Bear kissed him good night.
"Dozy, there's no secret to sleeping," Papa Bear said.
"You will nod off very soon.
But I'll show you a clever trick to help you.

"First wiggle the tips of your paws—give them a good shake.

"And now wiggle your ankles,
and now your knees.
See how *heavy* they feel.
Next wiggle your bottom,
feel it *sink*
into the bed.

"Wiggle your tummy. Wiggle your head.
And even your mouth and your nose. Now, see how
your body feels *settled* in bed, *ready* for sleep."

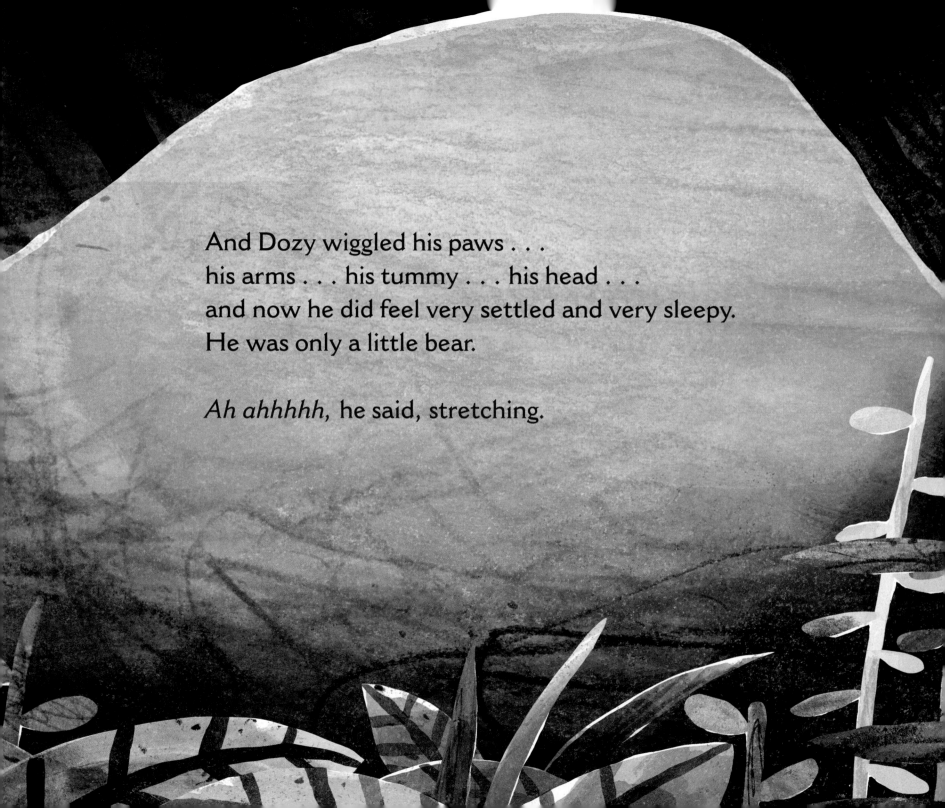

And Dozy wiggled his paws . . .
his arms . . . his tummy . . . his head . . .
and now he did feel very settled and very sleepy.
He was only a little bear.

Ah ahhhhh, he said, stretching.

"That's right, Dozy," said Nana Bear. "You're very sleepy.
Just stretch the last little bit out and feel how soft your bed is.
Feel how your body sinks *down* into it."
And Dozy stretched the last little bit out,
and felt his body sink *down* into the bed.

Down
      down
            down.

And he snuggled right in.
How cozy! The pillow
was so soft against
his cheek.

"Yes, snuggle down, Dozy," said Grampy Bear.
"And now hush and listen to the night."

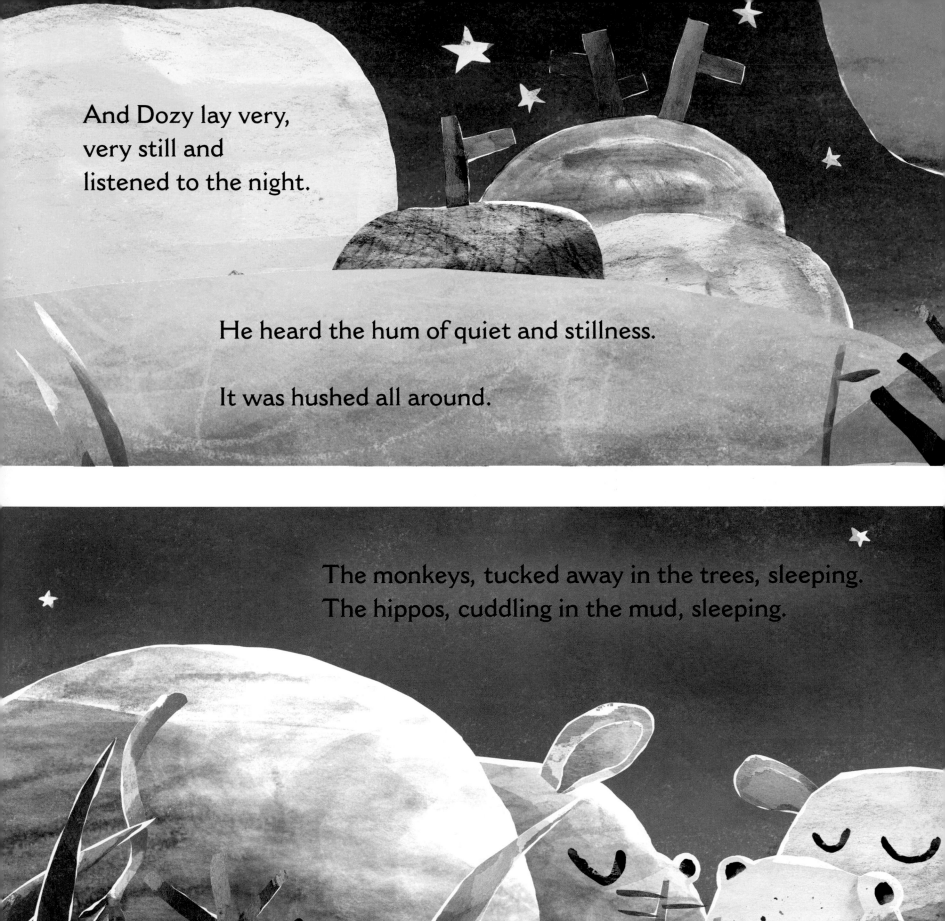

And Dozy lay very,
very still and
listened to the night.

He heard the hum of quiet and stillness.

It was hushed all around.

The monkeys, tucked away in the trees, sleeping.
The hippos, cuddling in the mud, sleeping.

The birds, high up in their nests, sleeping.

The giraffes, their long necks curled, sleeping.

The zebras, cozied up back to back, sleeping.

The elephants, softly snoring, sleeping.

Dozy's eyes were heavy. He closed them.
He shuffled down farther into his bed.
He put his little paw into the cool spot under the pillow,
and he listened to the night.

The silence wrapped him close like a blanket.
"Mama," he said.
Mama Bear kissed his head.

"That's right, little one," she said. "Quiet now.
Deep, long breaths, *innn—and—ouuuuuut,
innn—and—ouuuuuut, innn—and—ouuuuuut.*"

Dozy smiled.
The sounds of the night
hummed quietly around him.

"Hush," they seemed to say.
"Hush hush hush."
The secret of sleep was everywhere.
Deep, long breaths,
innn—and—ouuuuuuuuuut.
Dozy felt very quiet,
    very still,
        very safe.

The world of sleep swung him gently this way and that,
innn—and—ouuuuuut, innn—and—ouuuuuut,
innn—and—ouuuuuut.

And now he was asleep, a little bundle of sleep.
And now you can sleep too.
Only the sounds of the night, *hush hush hush*. . . .

Hush. . . .

Deep, long breaths,

innn—and—ouuuuuuuuuut,

innn—and—ouuuuuuuuuut,

innn—and—ouuuuuuuuuut.

Hush . . . only the sounds of the night.

Hush.